◆ THE TIME~TRAVELING TWINS ◆
Joining the Boston Tea Party

THIRTEEN COLONIES

(with dates of first permanent settlements)

Nova Scotia

Maine
(part of Massachusetts)

Proclamation line of 1763

Massachusetts
1620

Boston

New
Hampshire
1623

Rhode Island
1636

Connecticut
1633

New Jersey
1660

New York
1624

Pennsylvania
1643

CANADA

St. Lawrence River

Lake Ontario

Lake Erie

N E S W

Delaware
1638

Maryland
1634

Virginia
1607

North Carolina
1653

South Carolina
1670

Georgia
1733

Proclamation line of 1763

ATLANTIC OCEAN

BRITAIN

COLONIES

Boston

NORTH
AMERICA

ATLANTIC
OCEAN

Maine was annexed by Massachusetts in the 1600s and was not governed as
a separate colony. It became a state in 1820.

Vermont was claimed by both New York and New Hampshire. It became
the fourteenth state in 1791.

In 1790, when the first census was taken, there were 3,929,214 Americans,
of whom 697,681 were slaves. The Native Americans were not counted.

In memory of Jack Schultz
—D.S.

For Steve, Donna, Jenny and Michelle, with special thanks to Wendy
—H.B.

Text copyright © 2001 by Diane Stanley. Illustrations copyright © 2001 by Holly Berry. All rights reserved. Published by Scholastic Inc., 557 Broadway, New York, NY 10012, by arrangement with Joanna Cotler Books, an imprint of HarperCollins Publishers. SCHOLASTIC and associated logos are trademarks and/or registered trademarks of Scholastic Inc. 12 11 10 9 8 7 6 5 4 3 2 1   2 3 4 5 6 7/0
Printed in the U.S.A.   08   First Scholastic printing, September 2002   Typography by Alicia Mikles

◆ THE TIME~TRAVELING TWINS ◆
Joining the Boston Tea Party

by DIANE STANLEY *Illustrated by* HOLLY BERRY

SCHOLASTIC INC.

New York Toronto London Auckland Sydney
Mexico City New Delhi Hong Kong Buenos Aires

It was summer and time to visit Grandma.
We were so excited! Our parents think we like
to go there because we take walks in the woods
and make homemade ice cream and pick berries and
watch the stars. We do all those things, of course,
but there's something else we do with Grandma.
Something pretty amazing—we travel back in time!
It's a thing she does with her magic hat.
But you'll see.

We could hardly wait to have another adventure.
First we had to pick one of our ancestors to visit,
and change our clothes.

It's my turn!
I pick him!

Ah, yes—Ben Reed.
He was your grandfather's
great-great-great-grandfather.

Grandma went to her trunk
and picked out a black hat and two frilly caps,
knee britches and stockings, petticoats and
a couple of long dresses. It sure took time
to get dressed in the old days.

When we were ready, Grandma put on her traveling hat. We all held hands and closed our eyes. Soon that strange, dizzy feeling came over us, and all of a sudden we felt very cold.

We opened our eyes and there we were, standing on a Boston street. No cars, no fast food, and let's just say you could tell that the horses had been there. Just then a snowball flew past our heads! It hit the brick wall of a butcher shop, barely missing a soldier in a red coat. The soldier was really mad.

Hey, is that George Washington?

Temper, temper!

No, dear. He lives in Virginia. Lots of men wear powdered wigs like that. It's the latest fashion.

The boy who threw the snowball dashed around
the corner. Grandma told us to hurry up and follow him.
She said it was Ben Reed, and if we ran fast enough,
we could catch up with him.
We did, and he seemed glad to meet some "long-lost relatives."
He even invited us to stay at his family's house.

Ben's mother invited us in. A lot of her friends were there,
chatting and drinking out of pretty china cups.
She poured us each something from her silver teapot.
Only it wasn't tea—it was hot chocolate.
She said her club was called the Daughters of Liberty
and they wouldn't drink any more tea until England
stopped making them pay taxes on it.

But doesn't *everybody* have to pay taxes?

After the ladies left, Mrs. Reed asked Ben to show us to our rooms. She thought we might want to rest awhile before supper.

That night at supper we met the rest of the family.
Ben's father is a lawyer, and his brother, James,
is a student at Harvard College,
which even back in 1773 was 137 years old.
They talked a lot and dinner was fun,
but the conversation was better than the food.

They mostly talked about politics. Mr. Reed told us that for the last six years the British Parliament had been trying to raise money by taxing the American colonies. But the colonists had pitched a fit over it. They stopped going to stores that sold English goods. They wrote complaining letters and held lots of meetings. There were even riots. Finally, Parliament gave up on the taxes—except the one on tea. They kept that one just to make the point that England had the right to tax the colonies.

The next morning we woke up early.
It's hard to sleep with the clatter of cart wheels
on cobblestones right outside your window.
We got dressed really fast because it was so cold.

After breakfast Ben asked if we would help him put some notices up around town.
We said we'd be glad to.

Everybody seemed interested in our notices. Lots of people said they were coming to the meeting.

Ben said that Sam Adams had a big surprise planned,
but he wouldn't tell us what it was. We'd find out later, he said.
We could even be a part of it if we wanted.

Ben was right—the night of December 16 really was something!
Thousands of people had gathered at a church called the
Old South Meeting House. They were riled up, too.
We couldn't get close enough to hear all the speeches,
but we did hear one man ask the governor, Thomas Hutchinson,
to send the tea back to England. But he wouldn't do it.

Holy moley,
I never saw so
many people!

Yes, it's quite a crowd.
I'd say about a third of the
population of Boston
is here tonight.

Then Sam Adams ended the meeting with one short sentence. Ben said it was a signal.

We ran back to Ben's house, where he told us what was about to happen. Some patriots were going to disguise themselves as Mohawk Indians and board the three ships in the harbor. Then they were going to throw all the tea overboard.
We wanted to go too, so he helped us with our disguises. He told us to blacken our faces with soot from the fireplace and gave us feathers for our hair.
It was a very bad costume.

When we got to the waterfront, a group of "Mohawks" was already there. They looked as silly as we did, but we didn't recognize any of them either, so I guess the disguises worked. One of the men divided us into three groups and picked a leader for each one. We were assigned to the ship "Dartmouth." By the time we boarded, a crowd had gathered at the wharf to cheer us on.

I don't see any tea.

It's down in the hold. See that man over there? That's the captain of the ship. He's giving the keys to unlock the hold to Sam ... er, I mean, our Mohawk leader who shall remain nameless.

But isn't the captain upset that we're about to throw all his cargo into the water?

Sure, but he's not going to fight *this* crowd. He and the crew are going down below till it's all over.

The tea chests were heavy. To get them up out of the hold,
we used the ship's hoisting tackle and ropes.
As the chests came up, we hacked them open with axes
and dumped the tea over the side.
Soon the whole ship smelled spicy and sweet.

After a couple of hours our job was finished.
The captain got his keys back, and we even swept
the tea and wood splinters off the deck.
Then we marched off the ship in a double line,
our axes over our shoulders, while someone played
a tune on a fife. Everybody was in a jolly mood,
and the crowd treated us like heroes.
They even made up a song about us.

Rally, Mohawks!
Bring your axes.
Tell King George
we'll pay no taxes
on his foreign tea!

We thought Grandma would be furious when she found out where we'd been. But she wasn't. She said she'd read her history and knew that only one man, a carpenter named John Crane, was hurt at the Boston Tea Party. He was knocked in the head by a winch, but he soon recovered and walked home.

Well, my little ones— how did it feel to help start the American Revolution?

Is that what we did tonight?

Grandma said she thought we'd had enough excitement for one visit. Maybe it was time to head home. We were sorry to leave Ben—we liked him a lot! But we were starting to get a little homesick.

So Grandma got out her traveling hat.
When we were finally alone, we all held hands
and closed our eyes and waited.

And suddenly we were at Grandma's house on a perfect summer day.

Grandma reminded us that the next day was the Fourth of July! She said her garden club had built a float for the parade and we could ride on it.

AUTHOR'S NOTE

The Sons of Liberty threw 348 chests full of tea into Boston Harbor that night. When King George heard about it, he was furious. "The die is cast," he wrote. "The colonies must either submit or triumph." As punishment, the British closed the port of Boston and sent four regiments from the British army to keep peace in Massachusetts. Not only did this cause outrage in Boston, it angered the people in all the other colonies. United in their resentment of the British, they began to think of themselves not just as Virginians or New Yorkers, but as Americans.

At first they simply wanted to persuade the English to treat them with fairness. But gradually a new and shocking idea took hold: independence from England. The rumblings of revolution had begun.

On April 19, 1775, in the little Massachusetts towns of Lexington and Concord, the British army came face-to-face with the American "minutemen." This rag-tag collection of farmers and tradesmen who provided their own weapons, wore no uniforms, and could be ready to fight at a minute's notice managed to drive the professional British soldiers in their snappy red coats all the way back to Boston. Thus began the American Revolutionary War. It was to last for eight years.

On July 4, 1776, the colonies declared their independence from England. Seven years later, in 1783, the war officially ended. The thirteen colonies had become the United States of America.

—D.S.

THEN

lighting

1st flag of the USA

hair

dog

shoes and boots

hats

clothes

information and communication

It took 6 days traveling 18 hours a day to get from Boston to New York with a horse and buggy.

transportation

plumbing

cleaning and washing

clothes

hair

NOW

lighting

hat

shoes and boots

flag of the USA today

transportation

information and communication

cleaning and washing

plumbing

dog